APR 1 7

GREEN PANTS

Kenneth Kraegel

CANDLEWICK PRESS

Jameson only ever wore green pants. When he wore green pants, he could do *anything*.

He could dunk.

He could dive.

And he could *dance.*

Sometimes people tried to get Jameson
to wear pants of a different color.

But one way

or another,

Jameson made sure they didn't end up
in his closet.

One day, Jameson's cousin Armando came by with his fiancée, Jo.

Jo had the nicest smile Jameson had ever seen, and her eyes seemed to sparkle like the autumn sun shining upon a running river.

"Hey, Jameson, we have a question for you," Armando said.

"Would you like to be in our wedding?"
Jo asked.

"Absolutely," Jameson replied, staring
deeply into Jo's bright eyes.

The next morning, Jameson's mother said, "You know, being in a wedding is a big deal. There will be a lot of standing."

"No problem," Jameson said.

"And you'll have to smile nicely for all the photos."

"No problem."

"And you'll have to use your best manners at dinner."

"No problem."

"And *one more thing*," his mother said slowly. "You will have to wear a *tuxedo*."

"Okay." Jameson nodded. "No problem!"

"Jameson, the tuxedo will be *black*."

"WHAT?" Jameson gasped. "*BLACK* pants? *BLACK?* Are you sure?"

"Yes, I'm afraid so."

At the tuxedo fitting, Jameson rejected every pair of black pants that he was given to try.

But he was quite impressed with how striking his green pants looked with the rest of the tuxedo.

His mother, however, remained firm. "If you want to be in the wedding, you'll have to wear black pants."

The day of the wedding came, and Jameson still hadn't made up his mind.

"I'm sorry you have to choose," his mom said, "but I'm afraid you must."

"But how?" Jameson cried. "It's impossible!"

But all too soon, it was time.

"Okay, Jameson," his mother said, moments before the wedding began. "This is it. Have you decided?"

"No."

"Well, it *is* a tough decision, but I know you can figure it out." She kissed his forehead and went inside.

Jameson sank in despair. "But how? HOW? How do I make such a decision?

AAAAAAAAAAA

RGH!!!”

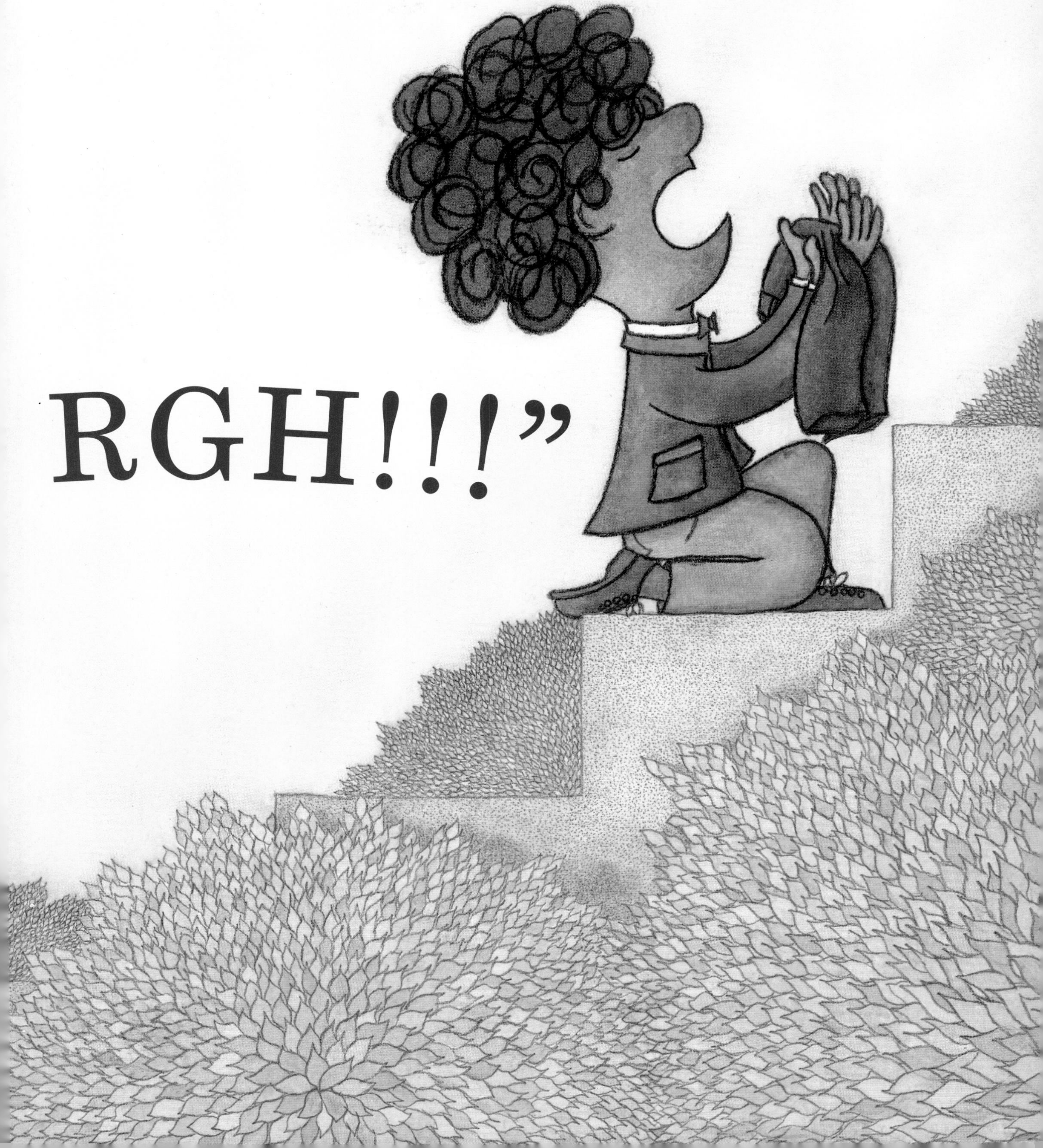

Just then, Jo appeared. Her hair played happily in the sunny breeze, her eyes shone like the summer stars, and her smile warmed his very soul.

"Hey, Jameson! I'm so glad you're here! I'll see you inside!"

And as quickly as she'd appeared, she was gone.

Jo's soft, sweet voice lingered in the air.
And in that golden moment, Jameson's
choice became clear.

The wedding began and Jameson appeared, right on cue—looking quite dashing in his tuxedo!

During the ceremony, Jameson stood very still.

Afterward, he posed for every picture with perfect charm and grace.

At dinner he was pleasant and courteous,
and his manners were impeccable.

But the moment the dance music began . . .

a pair of black pants fell to the floor . . .

and Jameson danced like no one has ever danced before.

For my parents

First edition 2017

Library of Congress Catalog Card Number pending
ISBN 978-0-7636-8840-0

16 17 18 19 20 21 CCP 10 9 8 7 6 5 4 3 2 1

Printed in Shenzhen, Guangdong, China

This book was typeset in New Century Schoolbook.
The illustrations were done in watercolor and pencil.

Candlewick Press
99 Dover Street
Somerville, Massachusetts 02144

visit us at www.candlewick.com